飄走的熱氣球

The Runaway Balloon

作者：珍奈特·卡樂
譯者：樸慧芳
插畫：林俐

高談文化

編者的話

　　當精緻的出書夢想，遇上了精緻的出版理念，會出現什麼樣的組合呢？您所看到的這本書就是在如此的理想結合下孕育而成。

　　高談文化素來堅持精緻出版的理念，無論在重點人物傳記、精緻藝術論叢、深度旅遊探索及英語學習等領域，都有頗受好評的出版成績，當本書作者與我們談及這一系列適合英國兒童閱讀的童話故事時，中英對照的出版靈光乍現於腦海中。

　　我們相信，在欣賞童話故事的同時，也能兼顧英語學習，豈不一舉兩得？而家長在陪同孩子閱讀童話故事之餘，也有練習英語的機會，更能賦予本書不同的功能，使全家大小都一同參與閱讀，讓讀書成為全家共享的一大樂事。

　　霹靂龍是故事裡的主角，他是一條由一名商人變成的印度巨蟒，天堂的守衛答應再給他一次機會，回到人間完成數件幫助人的善舉之後，才能夠進入天堂之門，於是這名商人以蛇的身形回到世上，經歷了一連串險象環生的冒險，而每一個冒險故事發人深省之處，都值得你親自去體會。

作者：**珍奈特・卡樂** （Janet Cullup）

　　英國劍橋大學教育碩士，詩人及作家

　　作品散見各報，詩作收錄於英國年度優良詩選多年。

譯者：**樸慧芳**

　　台大中文系畢，具多年編輯經驗，從事英語教學多年，目前任教於地球村美語中心。

插畫：**林俐**

　　本名林麗芬，自由插畫創作者，作品散見於報章雜誌與文學書刊。

飄走的熱氣球

1 又是一個稀鬆平常的日子，你知道的，什麼事都可能發生。霹靂龍睜開他的眼睛，發現已經是清晨了，他根本看不見太陽，因為一個巨大的七彩氣球正橫在他眼前。

「我確定它昨天不在這兒啊 ！」他自言自語地說。櫻花動物員來了許多遊客，在霹靂龍蜷曲的洞穴附近，豎著一個大牌子，牌子上寫著：

今天的特別節目
熱氣球之旅
兒童必須有大人陪伴

霹靂龍兩眼瞪得大大的，盯著這個又大又漂亮的熱氣球，在既粗且又結實的繩子另一端飛舞著。

他不禁回憶起自己還是人類的時候，曾經在世界各地旅行經商，坐著超音速客機，訪問各個不同國家的情景。

由於自己欺騙過很多人，而且愛錢勝過一切，當他死了以後，天堂的守衛不准他進去。後來守衛允許他以蛇的形體回到人間，做一些無私的好事以彌補過去所有的過失，守衛還答應他每做完一件好事，身邊就會開出一朵永不凋零的白花　，當足夠的花朵同時綻放時，他才會打開天堂的門。

一朵白色的花朵已經綻放在霹靂龍的洞穴旁，常春藤覆蓋的老樹上，標記著他曾經在祕密池塘解救過溺水的麥可。

黛西走進霹靂龍的洞穴做例行的巡視，黛西一邊工作一邊輕聲哼著歌，霹靂龍掛在一截樹枝上，隨著她的歌聲節奏搖擺。

黛西對他笑著說 ：「嗨 ！我的帥哥。」霹靂龍閉上眼睛，高興地發出溫柔的嘶嘶聲，因為從沒有人說過他帥。

黛西問他 ：「你喜不喜歡我的歌 ？」一面輕輕地撫摸霹靂龍頭上鋸齒型的霹靂紋。「你要不要聽我唱首歌 ？」霹靂龍點點頭「好呀！」黛西笑著說：「你真是隻聰明的蛇 ！我相信你聽得懂我說的話。」他當然聽得懂。

黛西拿著吉他坐在一塊平坦的石頭上，邊彈邊唱著甜美的旋律，霹靂龍則閉上眼睛隨著音樂搖擺，回憶著以前他在樂團伴奏下翩然起舞的情形。「啊！那個時候我雖然有錢，」他說道 ：「但是妳的音樂聽起來更美，黛西。」

突然，一陣掌聲驚醒了霹靂龍，睜開眼睛，霹靂龍發現人們在排隊等著乘熱汽球的同時，也一面在欣賞黛西的歌聲，並且給予熱烈的掌聲。黛西一陣臉紅，小聲地說 ：「待會兒見，我得走了，我還有好多工作要做。」她消失在側門後，只留下霹靂龍面對人群著的眼光，他立刻蜷縮成一團，把臉遮住。

不過霹靂龍對接下來的活動太感興趣了，所以裝睡也裝不久。這天的活動是為了改建動物園而籌募基金，霹靂龍很幸運能擁有自己的洞穴，但獅子卻需要更大的空間，動物園園長布朗先生希望牠們能有大一點的欄舍，好讓牠們能像在叢林裡一樣自由自在地奔跑。

「我知道什麼叫做自由，」霹靂龍自言自語：「獅子可沒有我這麼自由，牠們沒有水管或鐵絲網縫隙可以鑽出去。」每當夜深人靜時，他總會從這個縫隙擠出去探索外面的世界。他比任何人對這個動物園內的每一種動物、每一個地區都瞭若指掌。

10

他還知道管理員們想做些什麼，不過他也知道動物們的感覺，雖然只要願意就可以輕易逃脫，但他得完成足夠的好事以彌補他曾犯下的錯誤。

他需要白色的花朵好讓天堂守衛打開大門，除此之外，也因為他非常喜歡黛西。

「山姆，快來看這隻蛇，好大哦！」

霹靂龍的眼睛睜開了小小的一條縫，看見兩個淘氣的小男孩正朝

著他的洞穴裡張望，冷冷地說：「他們看起來真麻煩。」

「他好像死了！」其中一個男孩說：「我用這根棍子來戳戳看！

就可以移動牠！」說完兩個人都哈哈大笑。

霹靂龍睜開雙眼，剛好看到其中一個小男孩拿起一塊大石頭往自己丟過來。

旁邊的男孩喊著：「靠邊站！這樣會驚動他的。」霹靂龍倏地躲進老樹上茂密的長春藤中，像閃電般一下就消失了蹤影。

「當心！當心啊！他沒死！」男孩嚇得大叫，丟下
石頭和棍子，拔腿就跑。當然是去找沒那麼危險的
惡作劇，那並沒花他們太多時間。

霹靂龍在樹上，那個彩虹熱氣球在和他差不多高
的距離飛舞，繩子尾端離他的洞穴不遠。

他發現一個小男孩，手上緊緊地抓著兩張票，正往熱汽球
下的籃子裡爬，還幫一旁的小妹妹鑽進去。

就在他們的父母還來不及跟進去時，剛剛那兩個頑皮的小男
孩已把汽球上的繩子解開了。「住手！住手！當心！誰來阻
止他們啊！」

霹靂龍盡可能地大聲叫喊，只不過所有人聽到的只是「嘶...
嘶...」的聲音。這時，霹靂龍毫不猶豫地，朝那個在常春藤的

16

掩蓋下，不為人知的小縫隙鑽去，就在氣球從他的上方飄過時，
他用身子捲住那條繩子。

氣球愈飛愈高，他一臉驚慌地低頭看著下面的大海，風兒快速地
唰唰掠過，他緊緊地抓著繩子。

3「哇！」他說：「這和搭飛機可不一樣，現在我知道鳥的感覺了。」

突然，一陣強風把氣球吹得好高好高，遠遠地在動物園房子的上方。

「你要去哪裡？」高高的長頸鹿問道。

「如果我知道就好了！」霹靂龍一面回答一面抓得更緊，他們飄得比最高的樹更高，比所有的房子都高，飄進了天空中。

「鮑比！鮑比！我好害怕！」聽見小女孩開始哭泣，霹靂龍沿著繩子一股腦兒鑽進了籃子。

孩子們驚嚇得雙手緊握，睜大了眼睛。霹靂龍咧開大嘴，露出了自認為可以讓他們安心的笑容，並且對他們說：「嗨！別怕啊！我是來幫你們的。」兩兄妹嚇得不斷往後退，緊靠著籃子的邊緣，霹靂龍得趕緊想辦法。

21

「我該怎麼讓他們懂我的意思呢！」幾乎所有的人都討厭蛇，當他自己還是人類的時候也一樣，要如何才能讓他們知道他是友善的呢？

他突然靈機一動，小心保持平衡地用身子在籃子邊緣捲出：「我叫霹靂龍，我是來幫你們的。」然後舉起尾巴像手一樣要和鮑比握手。

鮑比小心翼翼地和他握手：「你好！蛇先生，我叫鮑比，這是我妹妹珍妮，她很怕生。」他解釋著，同時問道：「你要怎麼幫我們？」

籃子晃來晃去，珍妮哭了起來。「鮑比，鮑比，我好害怕，尤其是蛇。」

「別怕！珍妮，這條蛇跟別的蛇不一樣，他聽得懂我們的話，對不對？蛇先生。」霹靂龍點點頭說：「對。」

「你看！」鮑比既興奮又驚訝。

「他有魔法嗎？鮑比，」珍妮試探問道：「你說他會不會是王子，被巫婆變成一條蛇的？」

「別傻了，珍妮，」哥哥笑著說：「那種事只會發生在童話故事裡，這條蛇可是真的呢！哦…哦！」

籃子突然晃得很厲害，孩子們的手腳和蛇纏成一堆跌撞在籃子底。氣球直直地往上飛，霹靂龍皺起眉頭望著天空，天空又黑又暗，好像快要下雨了，強風迎面吹來，氣球也愈飛愈快。

霹靂龍鬆開尾巴，指著籃子旁的手把，示意要孩子們應該「抓得緊緊的。」他們也照著做了。

4　在遠遠的下方，街道就像絲帶一樣朝不同的方向展開，警車的笛聲夾著風聲陣陣傳來。

「你看，珍妮，那兒有一輛救火車，正跟著我們哩！」

當珍妮和霹靂龍朝著鮑比所指的方向往下望過去，看見兩輛火紅色的救火車，快速地朝氣球同一個方向前進。

然後，他們又看見一輛警車、一輛救護車和好多車子及人潮，整座城市好像都在為這兩個孩子及飛走的汽球擔心。當然他們並不知道有關蛇的事。

又是一陣強風把氣球往上吹　珍妮大喊：「鮑比！我們快要撞到那棟大樓了。」真的，他的　正前方直立著一棟高聳入雲的大廈。

25

「別擔心！」霹靂龍冷靜地說，

並且用力拉住其中一條拖

在氣球下方的繩子。

「抓緊！」鮑比大叫：

「閉上眼睛！」

結果氣球歪了一邊，從大廈旁

驚險地閃過，珍妮大喊：

「鮑比，你看！大家在跟我們招手。」

就在他們經過時，

人們靠著打開的窗戶向他們揮手。

「別向那些

人招手！」

霹靂龍發出嘶嘶聲警

告他們，他們很聽話。

26

氣球漸漸飛到了郊外，房子愈來愈少，有一大片空地在他們的下方。

「這兒倒是個降落的好地點。」霹靂龍心想：「如果我們不飛這麼快的話。」

「你想我們會撞到嗎？」鮑比問霹靂龍。「不會！」霹靂龍搖搖頭表示不會。

「那你知不知道怎麼讓汽球降落呢？」他很擔心。霹靂龍點點頭：「當然知道！」雖然事實上他一點概念也沒有，以前也從沒有坐過熱氣球，但無論如何他絕不能讓載著孩子的熱氣球墜毀，只要他幫忙就絕不會。

這時氣球的高度已經漸漸下降，掃過一棵大樹的樹梢。「哇！差一點！」鮑比嚷道。

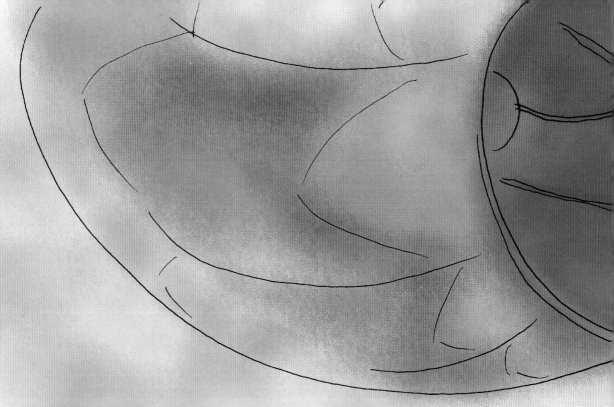

「想想辦法吧！請想想辦法，蛇先生！讓它停下來！」珍妮閉著
眼睛不停地流淚。

霹靂龍灰心地往上看，發現氣球的中心，有一條懸著的紅色繩
索，「對了！」他嘶嘶地叫，慢慢地用嘴往上拉扯繩子。

嘶... 嘶...嘶...，空氣排出的聲音嚇著了孩子們，鮑比因空氣
漏出的噪音而大吼：「嘿！這聽起來像是氣球破了，希望你知道
在做什麼啊？」

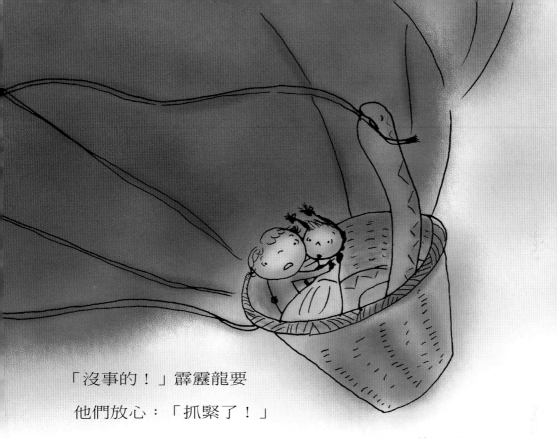

「沒事的！」霹靂龍要

他們放心：「抓緊了！」

「哦！鮑比，我想我們快墜毀了。」珍妮閉著眼說。

不過他們並沒有墜毀，霹靂龍一條繩子捲過一條繩子，又扯又拉地讓更多空氣排出來，最後終於降落在地面上。

碰！碰！碰！碰！他們落在滿是受驚牛群的柔軟青草地上。

「喲呼！我們安全了，妳可以張開眼睛了，珍妮，我們終於平安落地了！」

鮑比高興地跳上跳下，緊緊地摟著霹靂龍。「謝謝你，大蛇先生你太了不起了，我再也不怕蛇了。」

「我也不怕了！」珍妮害羞地微笑，跟著哥哥這麼說。

霹靂龍的尾巴末端因為高興而紅了起來，

他咧著寬寬的嘴微笑，深情地捲著兩個孩子，

不禁鬆了一口氣。這時他們又聽見了救火車的聲音。

「珍妮！你看！警車、救火車、所有的人都來了，多有意思啊！」

鮑比露出興奮的眼神開始數算車子的數量。「我們現在根本用不著他們了，這都要謝謝大蛇先生，你是全世界最英勇的蛇，我要告訴大家，是你救我們的，要他們以後也不要再怕蛇了。」

霹靂龍搖著他的頭，「不要！不要！這是祕密！」他的尾巴在嘴上作出手勢，要他們保守這個祕密，別告訴人家他和這件冒險有什麼關係，只是他們太興奮了根本聽不進去。

就在第一輛救火車趕來時，霹靂龍一溜煙地滑走，消失在草叢中，尋找回動物園又不會被人看見的路。
「哦！這個不錯。」他爬上第二輛救火車車頂的雲梯，輕聲說：「除非有人近看，要不然這倒是避人眼目的好地方。」
才一藏好，霹靂龍就聽到孩子們驚慌地對剛趕來的爸爸及每一個人，訴說有關一條勇敢的蛇讓氣球降落解救他們的經過，因為興奮而忘了霹靂龍要他們保守祕密的警告。

「這條蛇知道怎麼駕駛氣球，他真是了不起，他甚至懂得我們所
說的每一句話。」鮑比解釋。

「那他現在到哪兒去了？」他爸爸一邊問，一邊四處瞧著，霹靂
龍摒住呼吸，像木頭一樣動也不動。

「他剛才還在這裡。」珍妮大叫：「真的，他剛才還在這兒。」

「我們絕對沒有說謊！」鮑比堅定地望著每一個人臉上無法置信

的表情說：「你們為什麼不相信我？」他這兒看看，那兒瞧瞧，開始大叫：「大蛇先生，你跑到哪兒去了？」爸爸開始看來有點擔心。「一定是因為驚嚇過度，」一位救護車上的護士大驚小怪地嚷著：「過來這兒，親愛的，我們回家去，洗個熱水澡，然後上床睡覺，明天一早你們會覺得比較好！」

「可是，爸爸！」鮑比辯解著說：「有一條蛇......，為什麼你們不相信我？」

「夠了，鮑比！」爸爸嚴肅地說：「你會讓妹妹作惡夢，你明知道她怕蛇！」

「可是，爸爸，她現在不怕了！她......」

「夠了，鮑比！救火隊長特別答應，讓你搭他的救火車，走吧！在他還沒有改變主意之前，快上車。」

6 　鮑比猶豫了一會兒，看來是沒用的，沒有人會相信他所說的話，於是他轉身跑向火紅的救火車。

突然，他發現霹靂龍的身子纏在救火車的雲梯上，張大嘴正想喊出聲來，霹靂龍卻搖著頭，還用一隻眼睛眨了眨。鮑比也眨了眨眼，回應他還記得這個祕密。

就在這時鮑比對著霹靂龍舉起大姆指，珍妮則給了霹靂龍一個飛吻，然後匆匆跟著父母親回家了。

當人們正興高采烈地慶祝圓滿的結局時，霹靂龍已悄悄地沿著梯子爬下來，鑽進了被老常春藤覆蓋的洞穴，那個鐵絲網的縫隙裡。

「終於安全了！」他自言自語：「即使對我而言，這一天的驚奇也真是夠多了。」

黛西已經為他送來了晚餐，正在洞穴裡到處找他、叫他。他輕輕地從樹上溜下來，出現在她面前。

「哎喲！你嚇了我一跳！這是什麼新把戲？」她笑著對他說：「你躲到哪兒去了？我正到處找你呢！」

放下食物後她說：「今天真精彩，有兩個小孩被一個飄走的熱氣球載走了，就在那兒，他們已經獲救了！」她指著被開心的人群及放下心的父母所包圍的鮑比和珍妮。

「那個小男孩一直說是一條會駕駛熱氣球的蛇救了他們，小孩子的想像力真豐富！」

「可惜你一直在樹上睡覺，錯過了精彩好戲。」黛西邊說邊在又大又平坦的石塊上坐下來：「當然，」她笑了一下：「像你這麼聰明的蛇什麼都做得到，只要你願意又不那麼愛睡覺。」

她在霹靂龍的下巴來回撫弄：「我想明天報紙一定會登出來！」

「我想會的！」霹靂龍嘆了一口氣，開始吃他的晚餐：「真希望這是炸魚薯條！」

「又開了一朵，」黛西驚呼：「這些花到底是從哪兒來的？」她看著這兩朵潔白的花朵在樹上綻放著。

「還有一件事，」她疑惑的說：「它們不像一般花那樣會凋謝，第一朵花仍像剛開的時候一樣新鮮。我猜你一定知道這是怎麼一回事！」她看看霹靂龍，霹靂龍再次露出他一貫的天真無邪表情，咧著寬嘴微笑著。

「我嗎？」他發出嘶嘶的聲音：「我畢竟只是一條蛇啊！」但多特別的一條蛇啊！

The Runaway Balloon

It was going to be one of those days! You know the sort, when anything can happen and usually does.

Snapdragon opened one eye. It was morning, but he couldn't see the sun. It was blocked out by a huge rainbow striped balloon.

"I'm sure that wasn't there yesterday," he hissed. Then he noticed that lots of people had already arrived at Cherry Blossom Zoo and a large notice had appeared close to the pit where he lived.

TODAY
SPECIAL ATTRACTION
HOT AIR BALLOON
TRIPS
CHILDREN MUST BE
WITH AN ADULT

Snapdragon opened both eyes and stared at the huge hot air balloon,dancing in the breeze but secured by a strong brown rope.

He remembered when he had loved travelling the world when he'd been a man, flying in supersonic jets and visiting different countries as he made deals.

However, because he cheated people and loved money more than anything else, when he reached the world that exists beyond ours the Guardian of the gates of Paradise refused to let him enter.

Instead, the Guardian allowed him to return to our world as a snake to try and make amends for the wrong he had done by doing some unselfish deeds.

For every one he completed the Guardian promised a white flower would bloom and never die and when enough bloomed he would open the gates of Paradise.

There was already one flower blooming on the huge old ivy covered tree in Snapdragon's pit reminding him of when he'd saved Michael from drowning in the secret pool.

Just then Daisy, Snapdragon's keeper came into his pit for her first visit of the day. She put down his food and started cleaning, singing softly as she did so. Snapdragon hung down from where he was coiled around the branch of his tree swayed in time with her song.

"Hello my handsome man," she smiled at him and Snapdragon closed his eyes, hissing softly with pleasure. Nobody had ever called him handsome before.

"You like my singing, don't you?" She asked, reaching up to stroke the distinctive zig zag pattern on his head which identified him to the Guardian.

"Would you like me to sing you a special song?" Daisy asked and laughed when Snapdragon nodded his head and hissed, "Yes".

"You are a clever snake. I believe you understand what I say to you, don't you?" And of course we know he did.

Daisy fetched her guitar and sat on a large flat rock. She strummed softly and sang a sweet melody as Snapdragon closed his eyes and swayed in time with the music remembering when he'd danced to famous bands.

"I was rich then," he said "and I thought life was sweet, but your music is sweeter Daisy by far."

The sound of applause made Snapdragon open his eyes in surprise. People queuing for the balloon rides had also enjoyed the song and were clapping. Daisy blushed and whispered "I'll see you later, I have to go now I've so much work to do!" She disappeared through the side door leaving the whole queue staring at Snapdragon, who promptly coiled himself around and hid his face.

However, Snapdragon was too interested in what was going on to pretend to be asleep for long. Cherry Blossom Zoo had organized a fun day to raise funds for improvements to many of the animal houses.

Snapdragon was lucky and happy to have a large pit all to himself, but the lions needed more room. The head keeper Mr.

Edward Brown wanted
them to have a new larger
enclosure, so they could run
free like the lions in the jungle.

49

"I can be free when I like." Snapdragon hissed. "The lions are not so lucky, they don't have a pipe or a gap in their wire to escape from their cages."

At night and sometimes during the day Snapdragon escaped to explore. He knew every animal and every secret place in the zoo better than anyone.

Snapdragon was able to understand what the keepers were trying to do but he also knew how the animals felt now he was one.

Although he could escape if he wanted to, he needed to complete enough good deeds to right the wrongs he had done when he'd lived as a man.

He needed to earn the white flowers so that the Guardian would open the gates of Paradise for him and besides, he loved Daisy too much to just leave.

"Hey Sam! Come and look at this snake, it's huge!"
Snapdragon opened one eye a little. Two mischievous little
boys were looking down into his pit.

"They look like trouble," he said to himself.

"It looks dead!" one boy said. "I'll poke it with this stick!
That'll move it!" And they laughed.

Snapdragon opened both eyes in time to see the other boy pick up a large rock to throw. "Stand aside, this will move him!"

Snapdragon moved! Like a streak of lightning he shot high into the old ivy covered tree in his pit slithering deep into the leaves out of sight.

"Look out! Look out! It's not dead," the startled boys cried, dropping the stick and stone as they turned and ran away. No doubt to look for less dangerous mischief.

It didn't take them long to find it!

High in the tree, Snapdragon was almost level with the rianbow hot air balloon dancing and bobbing on the end of its rope close to his pit.

He noticed a young boy clutching two tickets tightly in one hand climb into the basket beneath the balloon and helps his sister in beside him.

As their mother or father were about to follow them the two naughty boys undid the rope and released the balloon.

"Stop! Stop! Look out, somebody stop them!"

Snapdragon shouted as loud as he could but of course all anyone could hear was a loud "Ssssssss!"

Quick as a flash
Snapdragon shot through the gap high in the wire that covered
his pit, shielded from view by the ivy and just as the balloon
lifted off passing overhead he twisted around the trailing rope.

As the balloon rose higher and higher Snapdragon gazed
down at the sea of horrified faces, clinging on tightly with the
wind rushing past him.

3 "Wow," he hissed. "This is a bit different from flying in an airplane. Now I know how a bird feels."

A sudden gust lifted the balloon high about the animal houses of the zoo.

"Where are you going?" called the tall giraffes.

"If only I knew!" Snapdragon answered clinging on even tighter as they sailed higher than the tallest tree, higher than all the houses, floating into the silence of space all by themselves.

"Robbie, Robbie, I'm frightened." The little girl began to cry. So Snapdragon slithered up the rope and dropped into the basket with a plop.

Both children gasped in astonishment, eyes wide with fear. Snapdragon smiled what he hoped was a reassuring wide, wide, snake smile and said, "Hello, don't be afraid. I've come to help you."

They backed away, very close to the edge of the basket and Snapdragon had to think fast.

"How can I make them understand?" Nearly everybody he knew hated snakes, he had when he'd been a man, but how could he convince them he was friendly?

Snapdragon had an idea. Balancing precariously on the rim of the basket he spelled out. "My name is Snapdragon I want to help you."

Then he held out the tip of his tail like a hand for Robbie to shake.

Gingerly Robbie shook it. "How do you do Mr. Snake? My name is Robbie and this is my little sister Jenny.

She's shy with strangers," he explained. "How can you help us?" he asked.

The basket wobbled and Jenny wailed, "Robbie, Robbie. I'm scared, especially of snakes."

"Don't be scared Jenny, this snake is different. He understands what we say, don't you Mr. Snake?"

Snapdragon nodded his head "Yes."

"See!" Robbie was excited and fascinated all at the same time. "Is he magic Robbie? "Jenny asked tentatively. "Do you think he's really a prince and a wicked witch has turned him into a snake?"

"Don't be silly Jenny," her brother grinned, "that only happens in fairy tales. This is real and .....ooohh."

The basket tipped sideways resulting in children and snake landing in a tangle of arms, legs and long, long tail in a heap on the floor.

As the balloon floated upright, Snapdragon glanced with a frown up at the sky. It was dark and gloomy as if it would rain quite soon. The wind was also blustery, blowing in their faces and moving the balloon along quite fast.

Snapdragon unwound his tail and pointed to the rope handles around the sides of the basket, indicating that the children should hold on tightly, which they did.

Far below them the streets of the city stretched out like small ribbons in every direction. then carried on the breeze they heard the sound of sirens.

"Look, Look there Jenny, there's a Fire Engine! Hey, it's following us!" Sure enough when Jenny and Snapdragon looked down to where Robbie was pointing they saw two bright red Fire Engines speeding along in the same direction as the balloon.

Then they saw a police car, an ambulance and lots of cars filled with people. It seemed as if the whole city were worried about the two small children in the runaway balloon. Of course they didn't know about the snake!

Another strong gust of wind buffeted the balloon causing Jenny to cry, "Robbie, we're going to crash into that building." Indeed they were heading straight for a tall skyscraper.

65

"Don't worry," Snapdragon said calmly, reaching up and pulling hard on one of several dangling ropes.

"Hold tight Jenny! Robbie shouted. "Close your eyes!"

As the balloon swerved and narrowly missed the building.

Jenny cried, "Robbie Look! People are waving at us." Sure enough people were leaning out of open windows to wave as they passed.

"Don't wave back," Snapdragon warned with a hiss and they didn't.

Now they had reached the outskirts of the city and as the houses became fewer large fields stretched out below them.

"This would be a good place to land," Snapdragon thought, "If only we weren't going so fast!"

"Are we going to crash?" Robbie asked.

"No!" Snapdragon shook his head.

"Do you know how to land a balloon?" Robbie was worried.

Snapdragon nodded his head, "Yes, of course!" But in reality he had no idea! In fact, he had never even been in a hot air balloon before. Whatever happened though there was no way he was going to let the balloon crash with the children inside. Not if he could help it!

The balloon lost height and brushed the top of a tall tree. "Wow that was close," Robbie yelped.

"Do something, please do something! Mr. Snake! Make it stop!" Jenny was close to tears.

Desperately Snapdragon looked up and spied a red cord hanging down from the center of the balloon.

"Yes that's it," he hissed, reaching up and pulling it slowly with his mouth.

Hissssss. The sound of rushing air startled the children.

"Hey, that sounds like a puncture to me! I hope you know what you're doing!" Robbie shouted above the noise of escaping air.

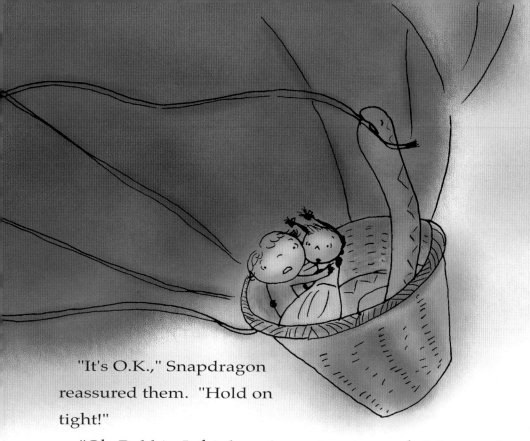

"It's O.K.," Snapdragon
reassured them. "Hold on
tight!"

"Oh Robbie I think we're going to crash," Jenny closed her
eyes. But they didn't. Instead, Snapdragon coiled from rope to
rope, pulling and tugging, leting out more air until the balloon
finally floated to the ground.

Bump, bump, bump, they landed on soft green grass of a
meadow full of surprised cows.

"Hurray! We're safe! You can open your eyes now Jenny,
we're safe at last!"

S Robbie was jumping for joy and
hugging Snapdragon. "Thank you Mr. Snake you were
wonderful. I'll never be afraid of snakes again!"
"Me neither," Jenny added, smiling shyly.

The red tip of Snapdragon's tail glowed with pleasure and he smiled his wide, wide, widest snake smile, coiling affectionately around both children and sighing with relief. Then they heard the sirens.

"Jenny look! Here come the fire engines and police cars and everybody. How exciting!" His eyes bright.

Robbie started to count the speeding vehicles.

"But we don't need them now thanks to you Snapdragon. You are the bravest snake in the whole world and I'm going to tell everyone how you saved us so that nobody will ever be afraid of snakes again!"

Snapdragon shook his head "No! No! It's a secret!" And put the red tip of his tail against his mouth as a signal for the children to keep silent and say nothing about his involvement in their adventure, but they were both too excited to listen.

So, as the first fire engine reached the field Snapdragon slithered away out of sight into the long waving grass of the meadow, looking for a way to get back to the zoo without being seen.

"Ah that will do nicely." He hissed and stretched himself out along one side of the ladder on the roof of the second Fire Engine. "Unless anyone looked closely this is the perfect disguise." He said satisfied.

Once hidden, Snapdragon was dismayed to hear the children telling theirfather who had arrived in the first fire engine and anyone else willing to listen about the brave snake

who had saved their lives by landing the balloon. They had forgotten Snapdragon's warning to keep silent in the excitement of the moment.

"The snake knew how to fly the balloon! He was brilliant! He even understood every word we said," Robbie explained.

"Where is he then?" his father asked looking around. Snapdragon held his breath and stayed as still and as stiff as a plank of wood.

"He was here!" Jenny piped up. "Truly he was!"

"We're not making it up!" Robbie insisted noticing the expressions on the faces of the adults.

"Why don't you believe us?"

Looking this way and that, he called out, "Mr. Snake! Snapdragon, where are you? Where have you gone?"

His father began to look worried. "It must be all the excitement," one of the ambulance nurses fussed. "Came along now my dears, let's get you both home for a nice hot bath and into bed, you'll feel better in the morning."

"But dad!" Robbie protested, "There was a snake! Why won't you believe us?"

"That's enough Robbie!" His father said sternly. "You'll give your sister nightmares, you know she's afraid of snakes!"

"Not any more dad! She⋯"

"I said enough Robbie! Now the fire chief says you can ride home with him in his cab as a special treat so off you go before he changes his mind!"

6 Robbie hesitated, momentarily, then seeing it was no use, none of them would ever believe him, he turned and ran toward the bright red fire engine.

As he ran he spotted Snapdragon stretched out along the ladder on top of the second fire engine and opened his mouth to shout, so Snapdragon shook his head and he closed it again. Snapdragon gave Robbie a big snake wink and Robbie winked back to show he'd remembered the secret.

They sped back to the Zoo, Robbie ringing the bell on his fire engine all the way and pulled up right outside Snapdragon's pit to reunite the children with their anxious waiting mother.

The crowd gathered to see the happy ending and Snapdragon managed to slither unnoticed along the ladder and dropped through the gap in the wire that covered his pit into the old ivy covered tree.

"Safe at last," he hissed. "That was too much excitement for one day, even for me!."

Daisy had brought his evening meal and was calling his name and searching the pit for him. Silently he slid down the tree and popped up in front of her.

"Oh, you made me jump! Is this a new game?" She smiled at him. "Where have you been hiding? I've been looking everywhere for you!"

Putting down his food she said, "There's been such excitement, two children were carried away in the balloon. There they are, they've just been rescued!" She pointed to where Robbie and Jenny were surrounded by laughing people and their relieved parents.

"The little boy says they were rescued by a snake who knew how to fly a balloon. . What imaginations children have!"

Just then Robbie turned and gave the thumbs up sign to
Snapdragon and Jennie blew him a kiss before they were
hurried away by their parents.

"Fancy you sleeping in the tree and missing all the excitement," Daisy said sitting down on the large flat stone. "Of course," she added with a smile, "A snake as clever as you could do anything if you wanted to and didn't sleep so much." She tickled him under his chin. "I expect it will be in all the papers tomorrow!

"I expect it will," sighed Snapdragon and began to eat his supper. "I wish this was fish and chips!"

"There's another one," Daisy exclaimed. "Where on earth are these flowers coming from?" She was staring at two perfect white flowers blooming together among the ivy on the tree.

"And another thing," she said puzzled, "they don't die like ordinary flowers, the first one is still as fresh as when it appeared."

"I bet you know something about this, don't you?" She looked accusingly at Snapdragon who put on his most innocent look and smiled his wide, wide snake smile.

"Who me?" he hissed, "After all, I'm only a snake!"

But what a snake!

單字解析：

1.

supersonic (n.) 超音速

例句：The two countries jets fought a supersonic battle.
兩國的噴射機打了一場超音速空戰。

pleasure (n.) 愉快；高興

例句：I have pleasure in being able to report that…
我很高興能向大家報告…。
It's a pleasure to teach her.
教她真是件樂事。

distinctive (adj.) 區別的；特殊的；有特色的

例句：This kind of rose has a distinctive scent.
這種玫瑰有一種特殊的香味。
What a distinctive cap you have got. I could recognize you easily.
你的帽子真有特色，我一眼就認出你了。

strum (v.) 撥弄；亂彈

例句：She strummed on a guitar while we are singing.
我們唱歌時她一邊撥奏著吉他。
He strummed on the table with his fingers because he was too bored.
他用手指在桌上亂敲一通因爲太無聊了。

melody (n.) 旋律；歌曲

例句：I just love that old western melody.
我很喜歡那支西部老曲子。
This is the most beautiful melody I have ever heard.
這是我聽過最美的旋律。

applause (n.) 鼓掌

例句：The applause thundered forth.
掌聲雷動。
He won a standing applause when he ended his speech.
演講結束時他博得全場起立鼓掌。

clap (v.) 拍手；輕拍

例句：Everybody clapped their hands.
人人都鼓掌。
He clapped the door to shut it.
他砰一聲關上門。

promptly (adv.) 迅速地；敏捷地

例句：They do things promptly.
他們做事十分迅速。
He turned his head around promptly.
他迅速地把頭轉開。

2.

improvement (n.) 改善；進步

例句：You may hope for an improvement in the weather.
你可以期望天氣會變好。
There is no improvement in the relationship between
the two countries.
兩國之間的關係沒有改善。

enclosure (n.) 圍繞；圍籬

例句：The lion has a very large enclosure.
獅子住的圍欄非常大。

mischievous (adj.) 惡作劇的；有害的

例句：Those boys are playing a mischievous trick.
　　　那些男生正在惡意作弄人。

streak (n.) 條紋；線條

例句：He ran so fast, just like a
　　　streak of lightning.
　　　他跑得像一道閃電一樣快。
　　　He usually gets up at the first
　　　streak of daylight.
　　　他通常天剛亮就起床。

lightning (n.) 閃電

例句：The house was struck by lightning.
　　　那房子被雷打了。

clutch (v.) 抓住；抱住

例句：She clutched her daughter to her breast.
　　　她將女兒緊緊抱在懷中。
　　　The boy clutched the candies and ran away.
　　　男孩抓了糖就跑。

shield (v.) 保護；遮蔽

例句：Please shield your eyes against the dust.
　　　請遮住眼睛防止灰塵。
　　　We must shield that girl from harm.
　　　我們得保護那女孩使她不至受傷。

trail (v.) 拖曳，拖著

例句：The boy was trailing his toy train by a piece of string.
　　　這男孩正用一條線拖著他的玩具火車走。
　　　He let the boat float trailing the fishing line.
　　　他讓小船拖著釣魚線在水面上漂流。

horrify (v.) 使驚恐；驚嚇

例句：I was horrified at the thought of that
　　　occasion.
　　　我想到當時的情景就感到恐怖。
　　　I was horrified at the news.
　　　聽到這消息我很震驚。

3.

float (v.) 漂流；飄浮

例句：Clouds were floating across the blue sky.
　　　雲朵飄過藍天。
　　　Our boat was floated by the current.
　　　我們的船被潮流沖得漂流起來。

astonishment (n.) 驚奇；驚訝

例句：Everybody looked at him in
　　　astonishment.
　　　每個人都驚奇地看著他。
　　　They watched the sight with
　　　astonishment.
　　　他們驚奇地觀看那景象。

reassuring (v.) 使安心；使恢復信心

例句：We were reassured that the ship was safe and sound.
　　　我們的船隻平安無恙使我們感到安心。
　　　His remark reassured me.
　　　聽了他的話我才放心。

convince (v.) 說服；使確信

例句：He tried to convince me of his innocence.
他試圖使我相信他的清白。
I cannot convince myself that he is dead.
我無法讓自己相信他死了。

wobbled (v.) 搖擺；搖晃

例句：Ducks went wobbling by.
鴨子搖搖擺擺地走過。
I wobbled in my opinions.
我的意見游移不定。

tentatively (adv.) 躊躇地；暫時地

例句：They tentatively answered my question.
他們躊躇不定地回答我的問題。
That shy girl smiled tentatively.
那害羞的女孩遲疑地笑了笑。

grin (v.) 露齒微笑

例句：He grinned broadly at me.
他對我咧嘴而笑。
They are grinning about something.
他們正對某事齜牙咧嘴。

tangle (v.) 糾纏；糾結

例句：The hedges are tangled with wild roses.
樹籬上纏結著野玫瑰。
The trees and bushes were all tangled together.
樹木和灌木糾結在一起。

blustery (adj.) 颳大風的

例句：It was a blustery winter day.
那是一個颳大風的冬天。

unwind (v.) 解開；鬆開

例句：She unwound the wool from the ball.
她從毛線團裡抽取毛線。
She unwound her arms from his neck.
她把繞在他脖子上雙臂鬆開。

4.

siren (n.) 警報器

例句：The fire engine sped past, its siren ringing.
　　　消防車響著警報器飛馳而過。

fire engine (n.) 消防車；救火車

例句：Here comes a fire engine !
　　　消防車來了！

ambulance (n.) 救護車

例句：I saw an ambulance speeding to that building.
　　　我看見一輛救護車朝那幢房子火速開去。

buffet (v.) 打擊；摧殘

例句：The boat was buffeted by the waves.
　　　這條船受波濤之打擊。
　　　She was buffeted by fate.
　　　她受命運摧殘。

skyscraper (n.) 摩天大樓

例句：The Empire State Building in New York is one of
the famous skyscrapers.
紐約帝國大廈是著名的的摩天樓。

outskirts (n.) 市郊；郊外

例句：My new house is on the outskirts of
Taipei.
我的新房子座落在台北市的郊外。

desperately (adv.) 不顧死活地；拼命地

例句：He made his efforts desperately to the shore.
他奮不顧身地拼命游上岸。
I need a glass of water desperately.
我極度想要一杯水。

spy (v.) 偵察；發現

例句：They spied out a secret.
他們查出一件祕密。
He is quick at spying the fault of others.
他很快就能看出他人的缺點。

puncture (n. v.) 爆破

例句：I got a puncture in my tire today.
　　　我的車子輪今天爆胎了。
　　　Our tires do not puncture easily.
　　　我們的輪胎不容易爆破。

5.

affectionately (adv.) 深情地；親愛地

例句：His grandmother stroked him affectionately.
　　　他祖母深情地愛撫他。

involvement (n.) 捲入；牽連

例句：My personal involvement with him and his family is deep.
　　　我個人和他家人瓜葛很深。
　　　This is the first serious involvement of his young life.
　　　這是他年輕生命第一次認真涉及的事。

meadow (n.) 草地；牧場

例如：There is a beautiful meadow around here.
　　　這附近有一片美麗的草地。

dismay (v.) 使驚愕；使失望

例句：We were dismayed by the violence
of his reaction.
他反應之激烈使我們很驚愕。
The boy was dismayed to see his idol
drunk.
這個男孩看到所崇拜的偶像喝醉了很失望。

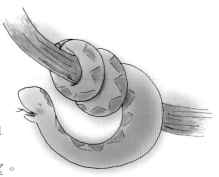

plank (n.) 木板製品；厚木板

例句：He doesn't move at all like a plank of wood.
他一動也不動活像塊木板。

protest (v.) 2抗議；提出異議

例句：They protested her remaining in office.
他們反對她繼續任職。
" No, you didn't say that!" she protested firmly.
她口氣堅定地抗辯道：「你沒有那麼說過！」

nightmare (n.) 夢魘；惡夢

例句：I had a nightmare about being
killed.
我作了個被人殺了的惡夢。

It was a nightmare to stay with her.
和她住在一起真是個夢魘。

6.

momentarily (adv.) 片刻地；短暫地

例句：The danger will increase momentarily.
危險將即刻增加。
I had momentarily forgotten.
我突然忘了。

wink (v.) 眨眼；閃爍

例句：He winked a warning to me.
他對我眨眼表示警告。
The driver's winking his lights, he's turning this way.
司機打著一閃一閃之燈光，表示他要向這邊轉彎。

relieve (v.) 減輕；解除

例如：Aspirin will usually relieve a headache.
阿斯匹靈常可減緩頭痛。
He smoked frequently to relieve nervous tension.
他一支接一支抽煙來減輕神經緊張。

imagination (n.) 想像力；創造力

例句：No one moved in the bushes, it was only your imagination.
沒有人在樹叢裡走動，都是你的想像力。
I don't think he is a writer of rich imagination.
我不認為他是個有豐富想像力的作家。

excitement (n.) 刺激；騷動

例句：It was a big excitement when Tom Cruise visited Taipei.
湯姆‧克魯斯來台時引起一陣騷動。

accusingly (adv.) 用指責的態度

例句：She asked accusingly about what
happened to my homework.
她責問我功課是怎麼回事。
My mother accusingly talked to
my father because he was late
home.
我媽媽以指責的口吻和我爸爸說話，
因為他太晚回家了。

國家圖書館出版品預行編目資料

祕密池塘=The Runaway Ballon／珍奈特・卡樂
（Janet Cullup）作；樸慧芳譯．－初版．－台北縣
新店市：高談文化．民90

 面　公分．－

中英對照

ISDN　957 0443-14-6（精裝）

　873.59　　　　　　　　　　90001193

90年2月15日 初版
發行人：賴任辰
社　長：許麗雯
總編輯：許麗雯
主　編：樸慧芳
編　輯：劉綺文 黃詩芬
美　編：林俐
插　畫：林俐
作　者：珍奈特・卡樂（Janet Cullup）
譯　者：樸慧芳
行銷部：楊伯江 朱慧娟
出版發行：高談文化事業有限公司
編輯部：台北縣新店市寶橋路235巷131號2樓之一
電　話：(02) 8910-1535
傳　真：(02) 8919-1364
E-Mail：c9728@ms16.hinet.net
印　製：久裕印刷事業股份有限公司
行政院新聞局出版事業發記證局版臺省業字第890號

飄走的熱氣球
定價:450元
郵撥帳號：19282592 高談文化事業有限公司